<u>Man of War</u>

By

Ron Brouillette

For You.

Sing, my tongue, of the battle in the glorious struggle.

-- Venantius Fortunatus

I

The salt from the water stung his eyes, and he closed them against the wind and the sting. He waited for a break in the air current before reopening them.

The water was a cold grey, with waves capped by dirty white. Near the rocks further below, it foamed and frothed, angry and agitated. The last words of dead men came rushing from the chaos, finding their way to his ears. Over the thunder, he thought he could hear words. Voices called to him from beyond, unclear. Thousands of voices warped into one deafening cry of the souls who were forever trapped in this place, bodies decomposing in the shallows, beneath the waves. Sailors and suicides, he was sure. From this place where he found himself, how many widows leapt to their fate? How many more took with them the children they shared with the men who had lost their lives in these waters?

Looking outward towards the horizon, the man thought that he may be able to see all the lost and forgotten. Squinting, he could just make them out. The families and those destined to spend eternity in isolation. Among them, it was not just the sailors, but the soldiers of wars, the victims of plague, and all the countless others who had fallen before the blade wielded by Fate and Father Time. From the distance, they called out.

But what words did they say?

Again, he closed his eyes. He tried to calm these thoughts, but in his thoughts were the waves. If only he could silence them, he could hear the echoing voices of eternity. He did not need to hear them, though. He knew what they called for. They called for him. Beckoning, siren sweet.

To my death, he thought. Or to further life. Perhaps neither. Perhaps both. What punishment would be worse? What more could they possibly do to him than he had already done to himself?

He opened his eyes once more. What more could they do to him?

The hike to the top of the rise was short, but hard. He felt the sting of each step deep within. Had he not completed this journey several times prior, the man would have thought to look at the scenery to take his mind off of the pain of the walk; but there was no scenery. The land was barren, only marked by grass too terrible for even a goat to feed upon, and the odd rock that lichen made home to. The land that faced the sea was no better for the life that called land its home than the sea, itself. A wretched, miserable place, this.

Weary, bones aching and muscles screaming, he reached the crest, and turned with one last glance to the sea. The cold glare of the water masked the spirits that had only recently plagued him. He knew he would not mourn leaving the place, only the solace it provided him whenever he sought it.

Carefully, the man readjusted the quiver slung over his shoulder, which was feeling sore and tender. He looked forward to unslinging this burden back at camp, relieving himself of the weight that had borne down through the pelt he wrapped himself in.

His fingers lingered on the fur. No longer soft, as it had been the day he had cut it from the animal which had been born wearing it, the weathering had made each hair tough, yet more brittle than it would have become had he left it in its place. He felt the bristles against his fingertips. The browns, whites, tans, and blacks all joining one another to become a color all their own.

How long had he worn this creature? Long enough to make it his own hide, it seemed. Even longer still.

Turning back from the sea, he eyed the path before him, and he found his heart and mind forever hardened towards what had surely seemed mystical and mythical when he was only a boy,. The grass, longer here than on the opposite face, was trodden from his many walks to this place; in some areas, the grass had been erased, replaced by bare earth.

Everything around him was worn down. Nature reflecting life; God mocking him. No, God reminding him. Reminding him that nothing, not even the earth upon which he walked, escaped the cold, unforgiving reach of time.

But this imprint the man had made would fade, as would he. The grass would regrow, and straighten back to the sun, all while his bones turned to dust. This was the world, as constant and unwavering in its way now as it had always been.

From where he stood, the man could not see the end of the path. As it stretched further from him, down the slope to where the world leveled and became flat once more, it turned and twisted just before disappearing into the trees and brush. It was as a serpent in the sand, winding between the overgrown mounds of soldiers from a different age who had fallen on this soil. Fallen here, never to return home.

When first coming to this place, and finding these hills the dead now called him, he was reminded of how close he was to sharing their fate on the fields of countries so far from his home. Even after moving beyond all of that, he was sure to find himself rotting to nothing in foreign places. Surely, this was the death that he had made himself.

But now, months after reaching this spot for the first time, the man's eyes drifted to the sky, and he saw darkness looming on the horizon. Night was soon to come, no doubt bringing with it another storm. Winter was setting in. The cold was coming. But the cold always came. Like time, the cold was always certain. It was the reprieve of warmth that did not seem as certain these days.

The fire was slow to spark, and it was barely more than embers when the last of twilight faded into darkness.

The stones circling him pushed the coldness back into his spirit as he blew gingerly on the coals, hoping they would spark the tinder. It would be a frigid night, and he knew he would need as much of the heat from the flame as he could coax forth.

As he wheezed the air from his lungs and onto the small flame that had grown, the fire began to swell, and soon he dared to add heavier wood and more bits of dry grass. The flames reached towards the stars that lay hidden behind the clouds, and soon he felt warm enough to loosen the hide and let the heat strike his skin. He rubbed calloused hands over his chest and upper body to push as much of the warmth into him as he could, all the while feeling the roughness of the years fade into the softer, newer flesh of the scars he carried with him.

An arrow to the shoulder.

Another near his heart.

Too many cuts, scratches, and scrapes to count or give space of memory to.

The man worked his rubbing fingers down to his stomach, tracing the reminders while massaging the husk that was his skin. So many reminders of things best long forgotten; so few tangible memories remaining to match the map that had formed on his body. There was a road there that had been well-travelled by the man, but he could no longer remember all of the stops along the route and why they were marked.

A glancing blow to his abdomen from sword or axe; no longer could he be sure, no longer did it matter.

Two more arrows below the ribs, maybe a third, or maybe just puncture from a stick in the brush..

A knife to his stomach, or perhaps it had been a spear gripped firmly by a nameless enemy on some unknown field of battle.

He closed his eyes, trying to remember that moment; that moment, and all of the pain that must have come with it. The joy of survival that surely followed soon after the sharpness had pierced him. He struggled to call to his recollection the eyes of the man who had embedded the blade into the softness of his belly, until hilt met fabric and fabric pressed flesh, or stick bruised the area around the wound, threatening to crush the last of him away. One thing he could remember with the greatest of ease was the warmth of his own blood saturating that which he wore, dripping out and down the hand of the man who dared try and remove his soul from this earthly realm. In the last moment, their eyes had locked, and no words passed between them as the dying man smiled, releasing his grip on whatever it was he had used to penetrate the man before him, believing he had killed his own killer with the last of his breath.

How wrong that man had been...

Opening his own eyes, the man wondered how long ago had that been. Ten years? Fifteen? Surely, not twenty. Surely.

As he traced the scar, he could no longer be sure. Time had closed the spaces it had once created, and now he could just remember the pale eyes of the man who had so nearly ended his life; fierce and strong, yet oddly welcoming. Death had lurked just around the corner, and yet there was no fear in those eyes. Even as the sharpness drained to a cold grey, there was no fear, and the only defiance found was for the man who ended his life, not for the specter who carried him away to ride the ferry.

A pop of an ember stirred him from his memories. It was time to eat, and then time to sleep.

The stew he made was bitter, but filling enough to calm the growl of his stomach. Green onions, strands of grass, and dried venison that would otherwise have been too tough to digest, let alone chew down enough to begin that journey. The first sips from the bowl burned his mouth and throat, but he appreciated the warmth that flooded within him and reached throughout the rest of his body, stretching even into his fingers and toes, travelling along his muscles and veins.

As the wind grew again, he stoked the fire, and settled in for the night, hoping for sleep.

The man's last thoughts, before his heavy eyelids collapsed upon themselves, and darkness shrouded his mind as it already did his body, went back to the soldier who had very nearly killed him. In the darkness of his thoughts, the man could still see the soldier's face: smiling, no sign of pain or weakness.

What was it to die? The man wondered this as he rolled, putting his back to the flame, feeling the cold from the stones on his face. Was it like stepping into a hot bath? Being wrapped in the arms of a lover?

Or maybe it was being stabbed in the stomach with either spear or sword. Pain and anguish, wrapped in the darkness of the infinite void. Only that, for all eternity.

The man shuddered in his soul, and then sleep found him.

She whispered as she asked him, When will you come home?

He does not know how best to answer her. A lie, to make her smile now and cry later; or the truth to make her cry always and forever more? His heart was torn over what to give her in the here and now; until, with great weight, he finally settled upon the lie. His silence, though, had betrayed the truth, and her green eyes looked away, full of a hurt that had been composed of rage and anguish, suffering and sorrow, madness and a hopeless acceptance of the fact that no matter what she did, no matter what words she could plead to him, his heart was as set as his mind was in this matter, and he would not stay with her.

She never wept for his departure; only a solitary tear would roll down her cheek as he gently touched her chin and turned her towards him. His hands, absent of callouses, would hold her softly as he watched her eyes for any sign that would give her away. None would come.

Slowly, he would wrap her in his arms, and together they would stand, neither wanting to let go until the other released first.

When will you come home, she would ask again.

Soon, he would reply. Soon.

There would be no smile.

The lightning awoke him, though he first thought it was the thunder. As the rain hit his face, he heard the last of the fire sizzle, and finally opened his eyes. The stars remained shrouded behind clouds. The storm had fully come.

The deluge was cold on his skin, colder than the night air that had wrapped his face in gentle embrace as he faded into the land of slumber. Still, he found it to be refreshing, and so he made no effort to cover himself. Even when cold, he somehow always felt at peace in the rain. It dared to come and try to wash away the filth, the pain. It dared to make things clean, and give the world a chance at a rebirth it did not deserve.

Once more, he closed his eyes. Deeply, he inhaled the damp scent of the storm. From the dirt and the grass came the smell of the worms and decay, purified by the falling scent of the clouds. Musty and invigorating, it signaled to him the end of the season, and for a moment he hoped to be carried away with the old. But the moment soon passed, and he was back in the cold and the wet.

Thoughts of continuing his sleep came to the man then. He was tired and it was a more than welcoming thought.

But then, he remembered the dream, and sleep was no longer seemed as welcoming as he hoped.

A flash of blue cut through his eyelids. Through the moisture, the air felt electric.

He waited, counting his breaths. They rattled out of him.

One...

Four...

Seven...

Twelve...

Where was the thunder? He kept counting, but there was another flash before there was a sound. He started the count again, more deliberate in his breathing. He kept it even, the rattle of his lungs becoming more pronounced. How these organs ached. A stab radiated upwards, through his ribs, reaching one of the scars – a bolt, slowed enough by what he had been wearing in that battle to not kill him. The damage, as he was too often reminded, was still done.

The man's lungs burned, and he was sure that death had finally come for him. Here, amongst the sacred stones, he had been found by that which existed only to extinguish life, and like the pagans of old he would die amongst them, but sacrificed to a cause he did not know, nor did he have any care for.

Another flash came before death, and the pain within him subsided. Where was the thunder?

The rain came harder, now; the deluge becoming a torrent. It was colder. He opened his eyes to slits and rolled to his side to look at the smoldering remnants of his fire. A pitiful mess of ash and smoke too stubborn to be washed away. There was no hope in rebuilding it this night.

Where is your valor? Where is your strength? For that matter, where is mine? He asked these things of himself before answering, As absent as the thunder is in this unholy storm.

What is lightning without thunder but impotent? What is a man without valor but impotent?

He needed to sleep, and he knew this. He had to find it within him, but the cold of the rain had ceased being refreshing. Now, it was driving into him. It pierced his skin and flooded his body and soul with unforgiving ice. The hide he wore began to stink with wet as the water slowly ceased to bead off of the brittle hairs and began to soak into them.

How long could such an unnatural storm last?

He stared beyond the smolders, past the stones that encircled this place once consecrated ground. In the darkness, over the grass, he could somehow still see the tree, existing almost as if only a memory. A silent guardian, it loomed at the edge of his vision, a black silhouette against the black of night.

Once, he heard a story of the tree. It was told to him by a man who once called this place home while the two were riding through a distant land whose name neither of them could pronounce.

The tree, the man said, is always bare. Never does it flower or give fruit. Never does a leaf grace a branch. It exists within its own shadow. On the hottest day, when the air is still and stagnant, it remains painfully cold to the touch, as though the breath of the Devil, himself, were gifted upon it.

The man paused as he said these words, and a shudder racked his body, as though his palms had fallen flat on the trunk.

When the shudder subsided, he continued by saying, The tree has been there since before my father's father. That old man once said, when I asked, that he could never remember anything hanging from its limbs, save for those condemned to it. For as long as any man knew, the tree had only meant death. There had to have been a time, my grandfather said, that life had graced the tree, for the tree was incredibly tall and impossibly strong, and that no tree could become ancient and worn in a complete absence of life.

Though I never saw a man hang from the branches in my youth, my grandfather told me that he saw several, as he would hoist those doomed to die after the rope had been wrapped round their throats and the priests had said those things they do to try and save the souls of those born only to be damned. He would stand, hands gripping the fibers so hard they would threaten to bleed, sweating and leaning back from the dead to hold them up. He would watch them dance until life was stripped from them, and keep them held until long after their legs had stopped kicking and their bowels released down their legs and puddled beneath their feet. Only then was he permitted to release his grip, dropping the soul-less husks into their own filth. The gravediggers would do the rest.

The man had taken another pause to survey the horizon that appeared between those before them.

When I say this tree is death, I say it has taken the life of those condemned to die upon its branches. It has taken the life, and is has perverted it. It is the opposite of life, and so it is death. It is soul-less, empty death. Whenever we march, it is what I see on the horizon. There, it waits for me. There, it waits for us all.

A light snow blanketed the world when he opened his eyes once more. The wind carried the loose flakes around him in a swirl; they danced like sprites during the solstice. Dawn was soon to break, and the clouds had gone; yet, despite the white, the world was a cold, unforgiving grey.

His breath hung around his face in a fog, and his bones ached terribly with the cold. He knew the time had come for him to venture further south, away from the frozen winter snow and to the forests of the lower lands, where cold rain and perpetual mist could haunt for the winter; away from this land of death, to a place of living ghosts. He could endure the cold rain amongst the trees far better than he could the snow in this open land.

For a moment, there was thought to restart the fire to gain warmth for the coming journey. The remnants of the previous flames were too solid, though; the few scraps of wood left unburned had frozen to the ground under a sheen of ice, topped by a light dusting of snow. He would expend too much energy trying to free it in a vain attempt to start the fire. Best to just gather his few belongings and leave this camp.

One more sojourn to the sea, then, perhaps? A chance to bid farewell to the salt and grey, and tell the voices of the damned that they would have to wait longer still to keep his company beyond the daylight hours.

This thought abated.

It was time to head south. No more wasting time.

The wind carried with him as he walked. Through his clothing and through the hide, he felt the quiver and bow on his shoulders. Their weight seemed to grow as his shadow circled him. On his hip, his sword, forever threatening to pierce the earth and drag him to the darkness below.

There was a time he could walk for days without rest, never feeling the weight of all that he carried. But sword and bow, quiver and cloth, were not the only things that weighed him down. The world, he knew, was changing, but he could not find the will to change with it.

The years had grown heavy on his mind, and he found himself now incapable of escaping the past. So many things done in the names of others, so many things left undone. How many had he killed? How many more had he left abandoned?

These were the things that filled his mind as he pulled the hide tighter, holding it with his hand at his neck. They were thoughts he wished not to have, but they refused to leave him in the slightest peace. In these moments, when he should find himself in harmony, they came to pick away at his soul; buzzards refusing to await his death.

How much more picking could there be before all was carried away, and nothing resembling a man remained?

He huffed at this notion. No man remains, he told himself, fixing his gaze on the road ahead, no man ever remains to be picked away. They are the scraps that refuse to die. May it be that the scraps do not know death has come, or may it be that they simply care not.

II

Geoffrey snorted as he ate the pottage. Tell me, Baldwin, he said, what do you know of what it is to long for home? We've been on this march since well before you were spat out by your mother! What you know of home, we know of as a mere memory, shadowed and disfigured by time. What you know of battle, we know as well as we once knew the thighs of our wives!

The men around the fire laughed riotously at this. The young man, Baldwin, turned crimson, and quickly filled his mouth with the bitter stew, waiting for one of the others to draw attention from him. It was true that he was young, younger than any of the other men seated on this patch of earth with him, and he knew they were only chiding him about his youth. Though youthful, he had already proven himself as worthy to be with them as any other man could. But still, the words cut him to depth he'd rather not know they could. He had earned his salt, and his place, but would he ever earn their acceptance?

Still, when the topic of his age and relative inexperience arose, he could not help but feel a sense of embarrassment that overshadowed the sense of pride he normally felt as he journeyed with the other soldiers. The worlds that they had seen, the victories that they had known. To be allowed into the company of such men of valor was truly a gift that had been bestowed to him. He supposed he should take the ribbing they gave him.

Now, now, leave the lad alone, a deep voice said from the other side of the flame. It's not his fault he has seen so few seasons, just as it is not yours that you have forgotten so many, Geoffrey.

Baldwin recognized the voice. Ralf was speaking. Perhaps the greatest of the lot, in the young man's eyes, he bore a scar for every fight he had ever encountered, and he bore them with something that many would call pride, but that Ralf would call wisdom. Truly a man to look up to in a life such as this, Baldwin was in awe that Ralf even cared enough to speak of the young man, let alone to speak in his favor.

And to that, Geoffrey, Ralf continued, when have you ever felt the thigh of any woman that didn't have four legs!

More laughter, much louder now, and Baldwin found himself joining in. Even Geoffrey had to smirk at that remark, and the bitter soldier gulped down what was left in his bowl, and broke wind in cunning reply.

Around the camp, all the fires seemed full of this life, a life that had been absent for the past several weeks as rations had run low, and tempers had flared higher than the flames of the fires. Though no battle had been fought, let alone won, in recent times, lightheartedness had crept its way into the men as they had found a village willing to give aid, even if they did not support the cause for which these men travelled and fought. For the first time in a long time, the bellies of the men were full, and so their spirits were high. No doubt such a bounty could not last forever, but for this time, this moment of their existence, it seemed as though it would be eternal.

Baldwin had even caught a glimpse of the King, himself, walking around the encampment with some of his knights, sharing in the good nature of the men he found. A weight, it seemed, had been shortly lifted from his normally brooding shoulders. Baldwin could think of no other time in the past year when the King had joined the men of the camp, and seeing him do so now helped to raise his own spirits, though he was not quite sure of the reason as to why.

The men of his fire continued to prod at one another, and through the flames Baldwin caught eyes with Ralf. The older man gave a slight nod, with a faint smile on his normally downcast face. So slight were these gestures that Baldwin was not sure if they were real or a trick of the dancing inferno, but the young man returned the nod, and then the gaze was broken as Ralf went back to the stew and to the company of the men who sat closest to him.

Alone in the wood, Baldwin stood, staring into the darkness that lay beyond the trees, lost in the thought of days past and futures yet to be realized. He thought of his mother and father, and of the village that he had born in. Though his mind longed for these things, for a life that he could no longer be sure was ever his own, he found that his heart did not share that sentiment, as much as it pained him. His heart was content with this place, with this life that he had entered into. Truly, this was his destiny; for were it not, would he find himself here?

Peaceful, here, away from the camp, is it not? A voice asked from behind him.

Baldwin had not heard the approach of any man, and was momentarily startled. The voice was one that he could not recognize, and so he wisely turned to see who was trespassing on his thoughts. Though it was too dim to see the man's face, the light cast from camp to his back silhouetted in clear the crown the man wore upon his head.

My Lord, Baldwin said, quickly taking a knee before the King.

No, no, please stand. There is no need to kneel for me.

The King's voice was refreshingly calm and surprisingly soothing, far different than what Baldwin had come to expect from the leader of an army and the ruler of a nation. For a man of such power, the expected voice would have been one of subtle fury and constant demand; but this was the voice of a father, offered to provide peace in a moment of quiet reflection, and not order in a time of chaotic war.

Forgive me, My Lord, Baldwin said, quickly standing, keeping his eyes to the ground, lest he cause some offense. He fought back the urge to tremble in the presence of his King. A struggle, to be sure, but one that he managed.

Silence passed between the two, Baldwin knowing not speak unless spoken to, the King sizing up the young man he found before him. Surprisingly young, the old king thought. He had been unaware that there had been new soldiers joining in this noble cause.

How old are you, son? The King asked.

I am sixteen, My Lord.

Sixteen, you say? Yes, that seems to be about right. How long, might I inquire, have you been riding with this army?

Nearly a year, Sire. I joined after watching a victory in the smoky forest.

The King held his tongue as he thought of that battle. The smoky forest was not a place that one could easily forget. The fire had been unintentional, but it had saved his army that day. Had the enemy not become confused and lost in the wood, The King and his men would certainly have made home on that ground until the end of times. Even without the thick smoke that the wind pushed into the trees, bringing ghosts to the battle, paths seemed to close on their own, and it was easy to lose bearing and come out in a clearing miles from where you had meant to find yourself.

Within his mind, The King could still hear the cries from the wood as he rode with his knights. A foolish maneuverer on his part, no doubt, but you cannot lead from the rear, and you cannot hold respect through such cowardice. How many men did he watch die that morning? How many others fell before his own blade that he was unaware of?

Over time, through countless battles, the numbers become lost, as did their weight.

Why did you join with us? The King asked, removing himself from his own blood-stained memories.

Your victory that day was great, and... and hard fought. I knew it to be the will of God that you continue to prosper and be victorious in your quest, My Lord.

The King paused, musing over those words. The will of God, you say?

Yes, My Lord.

Tell me, son, what is your name?

Baldwin, Sire. My... my name is Baldwin Rolfe.

Baldwin Rolfe, you say? Brave of you, indeed, to join with me at an age so young; chasing battle when you should still be chasing after girls who disappear in the sun. Might I tell you something, Baldwin, which I have come to learn about God's will?

I... I would be honored to hear, My Lord.

Please, look at me then, as I speak to you these words. I have found, through many years, and many battles, that the will of God is not often as we see it. You say that it is God's will that I claimed the victory in the smoky forest; however, that would be to say that God willed others to lose, and many on both sides to perish for a cause that is mine and my country's alone.

My Lord?

Please, hold your tongue. I have found that battle is not a will of God, and nor should it be considered such. I believe he has better things to do than to push the armies of men against one another, and to act directly in the death of so many men whom he has created. No, it was not God's will that the victory of that day's battle fell within our favor, no more than it was my will as a leader of men, or your will as observer. The will of the men sitting around those fires is the will that granted victory. Though they may fight for God, or wealth, or glory, it is not the will of those things that drives them, but their own will that drives them to carry on. Do you understand these words that I speak to you, Baldwin Rolfe?

Baldwin looked at the King as he thought on his words, and the King looked upon Baldwin as doubt and confusion were replaced by realization and acceptance in the young man's eyes.

Yes, My Lord, I believe that I do. It is to say, we may fight for God, or other things, but it is we, those who do the fighting, who decide the outcome of the battles we are part of?

Indeed, it is to say such a thing.

A knight stepped forward from the edge of the camp, and took a knee beside the King.

Yes, Elias? The King asked, his tone conveying that, as expected the disturbance may be, it was still a disturbance.

The knight stood, saying, Sire, the hour is upon us.

Thank you, Elias.

The King looked back to Baldwin, whose eyes were once again cast back to the ground. Think on these words, Baldwin, and know them well. It is neither God nor King that moves a man; a man can only move himself.

Baldwin went back to his knee, Thank you, My Lord. I shall not forget.

No, I expect that you will not.

The King placed a gloved hand on the shoulder of the young man kneeling before him, and there it stayed for a moment before leaving with the knight for his tent.

Baldwin remained on his knee, hearing the words of The King echo through the trees around him. The birds, the insects, and beasts remained quiet as he held his thoughts.

Young Baldwin, what word have you from the King? Ralf asked this upon Baldwin's return to the fire, steel eyes following the young man as he sat with the group.

The other men grew quiet hearing this, and all eyes fell upon Baldwin, who watched the King enter his tent with the knight, Elias.

You spoke to the King? One of the men asked, a hint of incredulousness within his voice..

No, I did not speak to the King. Nods and murmurs traced their way around the fire. The King, Baldwin said, his voice rising, spoke to me.

The same thought echoed through all of the men present: Why had their king spoken to Baldwin, who is barely but a boy? What could he know that they did not, and what was it the King wanted to know?

Baldwin could feel the eyes of the others on him. He felt that there was no qualm about his age any longer. They all wanted to hear the story, know the words that had been spoken. For this point in time, he was more than their equal – he was a man who had spoken to a king; something none of them had done on their lengthy journey.

Baldwin looked into the flames. Through them. He saw Ralf looking at him, a wry smile played out across his face. The scars he carried now seeming to fade in the flicker and dance of the fire. The axe wound that ran through his hairline all but vanished. Of the men giving rapt attention, Ralf's was the attention he most craved. The most battle-worn, world-weary of these soldiers now had an unbroken focus on the boy. He wanted to hear, perhaps more than the others, what it was that Baldwin would tell them.

The flames cracked, and somewhere, at another fire, music and laughter reached their ears. Baldwin would tell Ralf his story. He would tell all of these men his story.

III

The doe walked slowly. To an observer, she seemed to be wandering aimlessly, but with each step, there was a greater purpose. Every motion was meant to ensure survival. Hardly a sound was produced when she moved. She was the epitome of grace and elegance as she foraged in the woods. Occasionally, her head would raise up. The deer would look around, for predators and for a quick escape if she felt it time to flee. After this pause, she would return to foraging, and no one would be the wiser.

In her fourth winter season, the animal had become adept at the survival game. She had escaped poachers and wolves, arrows and eagles. Living was her only true purpose during these times.

She served this purpose well.

A rustle in the brush caught the doe's attention, and she froze, head held high, eyes looking to the source of the sound. She waited, her heart hammering within her chest, body preparing to run if the situation called for it. Any sign of movement would give away the danger.

A thousand beats of the animal's heart reverberated through the wood. No movement seen, no other noises heard. Safety, perhaps?

She continued to wait.

The man watched the animal stare at him. He held perfectly still, willing his arms not to shake as they continued to hold the bowstring, arrow drawn as far back as it could go. He knew that the slightest twitch in the smallest muscle would cost him this moment, and the hunt would then begin anew. He couldn't have that. Not now. Not this time.

He had been stalking the doe since first light; had almost lost her more than once. There had been times when he was sure that he had. But then, almost without trying, he would find her, walking, still moving gracefully through the undergrowth. She kept to the areas of safety, seeming to know them as well as he knew the tattered map that was his own body. The thickets of shrub, the places between the hawthorn; these were the spots she could feel at peace. The occasional light brown against an endless sea of moist green – the only thing that distinguished her from the surroundings.

Each step of hers placed lightly on the damp moss. No prints ever left behind. Harder to track. Still, he had managed, and the man had finally been able to place her in his sight. The arrow was on her chest. He pulled the bowstring back, and it caught what could barely be considered a twig.

The wood did not snap, but the tree rustled, and she had heard it. She found his position with her gaze. The world froze as they waited for one another make the next move.

He knew that if he let fly while she stared at him she would be gone before the arrow reached its target. Patience became the new game they played.

The doe continued to listen. The silence almost becoming too much. Neither bird nor bee made noise amongst the trees and brush. Just the calm of the wood, hiding a secret from her.

This was nothing new to her. She could wait to find out what secrets were being kept in the world around her.

The light moved around the wood with the sun. His mouth felt parched, though the air was thick with moisture. His shoulder and knuckles ached. His legs burned. His stance was becoming painful. Every grain of sand that dropped in the hourglass froze in free-fall.

One of them had to lose this game. It would not be him

He was not sure how much longer he could last.

Perhaps the doe was wrong. Perhaps there was nothing there. A bird had made the noise. The water had grown too heavy on a leaf, and it had given way, the weight on the branch lessened, and so it could rise slightly higher.

Her instincts, though, told her this was not the case. As possible as these things were, they were not probable. Experience in this life had taught her to never believe in the banal of the world; always expect that which is most dangerous to be the truth of a situation

She sniffed the air, hoping for a strange scent to flood her nostrils and give away that which waited for her. Any smell at all to give away the pursuer that had been following her. After several inhalations, nothing came to her but the scent of the wood and her own wet fur.

Slowly, she lowered her head, adjusting her gaze. She was not ready to lay down her guard. From this angle, with her eyes lower, she could see the shadows differently. From this perspective, she could better see if they moved.

The day felt as though it passed into night. Night felt as though it passed into day. Seasons were changing and changing back. He could feel his bones turn to dust beneath his flesh as time played its own game, one that would last longer than the game he played with the animal he was hunting.

He watched her lower her head, and thought this may be the moment, the last chance that he would have at her; but her eyes never left him. They pierced into his chest, through his heart, and out his back, gaze shooting through the forest as his arrow should shoot through her heart. She saw him with the wood, man and nature becoming one. Of this he was sure, and that was all that kept her with him.

Measuring his breathing, he willed himself not to count the seconds. He was a man who knew time too well. Waiting for the assault, burying a brother, watching the stars circle in the heavens; everything was about time, and time was eternal.

But he was not. Neither, it turned out, was their game.

A thrush lifted from the growth behind him. The hawthorn shook, the air pierced by its song. For a instant, he glanced at the bird with eyes alone, willing it a soundless death, cursing it forever into whatever life it may next find itself in.

She was gone when his eyes returned forward, looking down the arrow.

He stayed his shot.

Fool, he thought to himself. Old fool. You should have known. You should have taken your shot! Now, your belly will remain empty of meat!

But he knew better. Had he let fly the arrow he had drawn, he would be just as hungry at his return to camp, only he would be more drained of energy after wasting it on a hunt for his arrow in the underbrush.

He sank the arrow back into the quiver.

In anger, he broke the initial cause for distraction, the small branch snapping easily in his hand, completing the work on the tree his bowstring had begun. Slumping in the cold, wet moss, he let his body mend itself of the pain his too-long-held stance had caused him before going on his way.

That night, he heard the wolf before he saw it. Not a howl or a bark carried through the darkness to him, but the unmistakable sound of padded paws, walking slowly over earth and stone, gave way that he had a visitor in the night. The meticulous patter was the unmistakable sound of a predator stalking potential prey..

He sat near his fire, shoulders slumped. The flames danced and told him a story of long ago. The story of a king, and the words he said to a young boy on the edge of a camp of soldiers. What were those words that had once been spoken? He wondered this as he ate his foul stew.

The man's first glance from the flame revealed the faces of his comrades. Soldiers. Men. His brothers. They were solemn and empty, though; not how he chose to remember them. Faces of the dead, eyes as white as mother's milk, and forever unblinking. The wounds that killed them remained open on their bodies. So, they had followed him from the oceans of the North. Surely, they wondered why he was not with them. As the man often did, he wondered the same.

Through the flame, he saw the face that haunted him the most. When the others had all taken their leave, this was the face that remained, keeping him company well beyond the witching hour. He closed his eyes, willing it to go away. That's when he first heard the wolf.

Opening his eyes, all of the dead men were gone; yet, their presence still remained.

The wolf had been stalking him for more than a week, but it was not the stalk of the hunt. It seemed to only be interested in the man who had come from the North, shrugging cold and snow from his shoulders as he entered the wolf's territory, only to have it replaced by new cold and rain of the South.

The man had first caught sight of it through the trees far from the edge of the clearing he had been crossing. The creature's fur was black as the moonless night, and it had been staring at him. It had remained still, just beyond the reach of his arrow, and posed no real threat at the time. He had felt no need to pursue it further. Though the pelt would keep him warm and the meat would keep him full, it had been his experience that tracking and killing a wolf was far more effort than it was ultimately worth; so, he let the creature live.

Still, he coveted the long fur that coated the animal. He knew it would serve him better than the ancient deer that he currently wore. In time, maybe he would seek the wolf out; however, he needed to first find easier prey in the form of a deer. The wolf was a secondary concern.

He had been surprised not to find the animal in the wood earlier as he had held the deer at the tip of his arrow. If anything would have scared the doe away, it would have been the wolf, which the man had taken to calling Tristan, for lack of a better name.

Over the course of the week, he had learned to appreciate Tristan's infrequent companionship. Often, when the wolf came to him at night, staying just beyond the flicker of the fire so only the beast's eyes would glow in the shadows; embers unto themselves. He would find himself speaking to it as the animal were a long forgotten friend. Indeed, on a night when the dead came to visit him, Tristan was a friend, there to keep the darkness at bay, even if that is where both the animal and the man preferred to live.

Someday, Tristan, you'll join their ranks, and when I look around this fire, I'll see you, sitting with them, hollow, no more real to me than you are now, he said to the floating embers that peered at him from the shadows.

He slurped at his stew, filtering out the grass with his teeth and flicking the blades to his feet.

Would the animal allow him, he would share the meal; however, he had tried that once already, and Tristan had fled further into the dark of night, not to return until the following evening.

A guardian or a devil, the man continued to wonder at the animal's purpose in following him. Surely, after a week of constant moving, this night being the first he had kept camp in the same place, the pair had ventured far from Tristan's home. What need did the wolf have in following him further south? Curiosity, perhaps, or maybe the wolf sensed death upon the man, and was waiting for the opportunity of a hunt-less meal.

If it is death that brings you to me, Tristan, know that it follows me wherever it is I roam. I cannot shake it as you would shake the rain from your coat. It is ever my companion, more so than you are these bleak days. Nay, I would say that the death you await from me is still long in coming, for that would be my curse.

The man thought over these words he spoke to the animal. A truth he had accepted without much thought, now he began to dwell upon it. Why had death refused to carry him to the ferry, where it had taken all of those he had known before? Why had it stayed its hand on the fields of so many battles, only seeming to leave him, now, as the last man standing?

How could he have committed so terrible a wrong to warrant such a punishment as this?

Maybe that is why Tristan had found him; to force him to think about such things.

Where is the child? Her voice called to him from the other room.

He called back to her, asking what child it was that she spoke of, for they had none.

Where is our child?

Her voice was empty and detached, drifting to his ears like a ghost on the wind. He left what he had been doing and went into the room to find her.

We have no child, he said again. There was an urgency in his voice he did not know. Pain in his words.

She stood in the room, her bare back to him. Before her, there was only empty space and then the stone of the wall. Everything about this place felt cold. Her skin was pale and without blood, and her once glorious black hair flowing loosely and muted.

My love, he said to her, are you all right?

Where is our baby?

Her call was mournful, and unearthly. It hurt him to hear it, and pained him further to say again that they had no child, for their child had died before it had ever lived, and they had not been blessed with another, and likely never would.

He approached her, placing his hand on her shoulder, and quickly drawing it back. She felt of ice, and his fingers burned from the chill.

My love, you are so cold. Please, let me fetch you a blanket.

I want my child.

My love…

I want my…

She turned to face him, and he fell back onto the floor, terror forcing his heart to beat in madness at what he saw, and what he knew could not be real.

His beloved stood before him, naked and white as stone; her eyes rolled back, and her mouth agape, the earth from where their newborn son had been buried spewing from her mouth. This soil still held the worms that feasted upon the dead infant.

…child.

Her voice was no longer mournful, but guttural. There was an unholy fury to be found within her words.

As she stepped towards him, he could only stare in horror. The shock of her, appearing to be as dead as their child, rooted him in place.

She stopped moving, holding herself over him, the pale orbs, laced with veins, devoid of pupils, stared into him, threatening to suck whatever life force remain within him from his body.

I want our child, she said, spewing the rotted earth upon him.

Panicked, he brushed away the worms and dirt, but still stay on the spot he had found when falling. He watched her as she pushed her fingers into the flesh of her belly, black blood spilling out. Her arms sank deep within her, farther than should be possible.

And then he heard a child's cry.

Slowly, she pulled her hands out, clasping a black, quivering mess that mewed like an infant, before screeching so loud the walls cracked and the floor shook beneath him.

Now we are a family, she said, cradling the creature to her breast, where it suckled death from her.

The air was thick as he gasped it into his lungs. Though each panted breath hung before him in clouds in the cold air, the sweat on his skin was hot and blistering. He lunged forward onto his hands and knees, body retching, vomit forming a puddle in the mud around his fingers.

From a distance, the wolf, without sympathy, watched the man shudder in the predawn hours near the smoldering remains of his fire.

IV

The men had left the green behind, and found themselves marching on rocky terrain that was alien and unforgiving. Under a never setting sun, each man longed for a cloud, some rain, or the wetness of the ocean. Though the army moved from water source to water source, the days in between made the journey agonizing, and it never was long before the lot felt sorry and parched for thirst. The sand that coated the rocks seemed to dry their tongues and spill from their mouths in heaps.

It appeared to all that God had cursed these lands.

The good nature that Baldwin had shown two years before was gone, replaced by a pragmatism that seemed to be beyond his years. After many battles fought, and many brothers in arms lost, he was no longer chided by the group for his youth and inexperience, but was welcomed into their solemn comradely, for he had seen what they had seen, carried the scars that they carried. He now knew what it was to gaze into the eyes of another man as he was impaled on the edge of the sword; what it was to have the blood of the enemy soak his skin and bathe his face, and the saltiness that was brought with it; and he knew all too well the burden it placed on the soul to take the life of another man, even if that man be found an enemy, and how the memory of the kill never faded, but only became more focused, over time. Beyond this, these years on, more than one occasion had past where he had proven himself more than equal to those with whom he marched, just as they had proven themselves to him.

It could be said, without second thought, that the years had been hard on the man. Yet, of the scars that Baldwin now found him himself bearing, the worst had just formed; a wound the width of his body that stretched across his back from a sword on a field that had surely been as forgotten by God as this forsaken new land he now found himself in. He still walked with a grimace as he adjusted to the new found tightness of the flesh, but was pleased there was no longer pain as sweat slipped down his back to the spot of the injury, trickling into the gash with taxing sting.

These days, each step caused him a myriad of pains; if they were not to be found in the soles of his feet from the broken, unforgiving surface of the terrain, then they would lurk within his knees, hips, and spine. Bones ached as they rubbed against bones, flesh felt sore from sun and blade, and even his very blood seemed to hurt as it pulsed within his veins. Baldwin had grown to feel as though he were a man of a thousand years. He longed to ride upon a horse with some of the other men he had come to call his brothers, if only to relieve himself of the ever growing burden that was his body. He hoped to find one soon, as Ralf had done after a battle not long ago that somehow seemed little more than a distant memory.

Even after battle, the warrior had said, riding to Baldwin or the trodden grass and soil that leaked the blood of the men of who had fallen, there is mercy in the act of appropriation.

It is a fine beast, Baldwin had told his friend, wrapping his hand in cloth to stop the bleeding from a blow that hand landed too near a point of removing his fingers than he was comfortable with.

He is more than a fine beast, young Baldwin. An animal that goes with you to war is a companion. Just as you are my friend and brother, so may this beast, as you falsely seem fit to call him, be to me. He will carry me into battle, and hopefully into the next one after. I will burden him as we travel, and, in turn, I shall protect him, as I would protect the next man at my side. Do you understand what it is I am telling you?

Baldwin looked up at the great man, sun shining a halo upon the crown of his head. The heavenly lie nearly hid the blood of enemies that covered his face, causing it to appear as little more than dirt and grime. You are telling me that you have stolen a companion, and as there is no maiden for you to love, you have chosen a horse to take her place.

Ralf frowned at that, saying, Be careful when speaking to a man about what he loves, Baldwin. Love and loss walk hand in hand for men like us, and loss always leads the way.

The young man looked to his feet, having forgotten his place, and forgotten those with whom he was with. I'm sorry, my friend, I did not think–

No, you did not, and I hope such a mistake never finds you again.

With that, Ralf rode away, good nature and swagger of victory pulled from him, a shadow holding tight across his face. Baldwin watched him go, forgetting of the mending that his hand required. What words had he said to upset Ralf so, he wondered. What is the loss he speaks of?

It was not uncommon for words of a similar nature to be thrown about around the flame of a camp, but they were always taken in the jest they were spoken with. Here, however, they seemed to have nearly broken a man. For that, Baldwin felt shame.

The ambush came as one would expect. Along the rocks, within a gorge, the men marched in a bumbling fashion. There was no real order and form among the ranks. They had marched, and they had marched, and then then they had marched some more. Though they never knew the battlefield before they found it, they had never seemed to have been challenged while sampling marching. Always, they had awoken at camp, been told to grab their weapons and armor, and had then pressed forward to a wall, a bridge, or something that, for whatever reason be, needed to be claimed by them.

When the ambush fell upon them, there was no cry of attack. No call from the enemy to give away their purpose, or even their very presence. The first sign came when an arrow struck the rider next to Ralf as Baldwin walked closely, listening into their conversation. As the man spoke of death, he found himself within its throws, and sliding from the horse, bleeding like a stuck pig, gurgling as his lungs filled with the blood that he would drown in, he was soon to be no more.

Baldwin continued moving his feet with the other men for three more steps, surprised at the figure sliding from the saddle with an arrow in his chest, blood wheezing from the wound and from his mouth. Ralf bellowed a call to all the men in line, jumping from his horse as he did so, slapping its hindquarters as he landed to send the creature running. His voice carried like thunder up and down the gorge, so that all within sight, and even those further away, heard it and took heed. In a deft maneuver, he grabbed the collar of the young boy and drug Baldwin to the rocky earth beneath them as more arrows appeared in the sky. Like larks, Baldwin thought as he watched them arc across the space over their heads. So many they could nearly block the sun itself, and turn day to night.

Ralf's call to arms did little to save many from the first onslaught. Those who had been chosen to die fell, grasping at the sticks that jutted forth from them. More fell wounded, an arrow in the leg pinning them to a horse, or one in the arm that would prevent them from raising a sword. Shots of skill or luck, it was hard to know from the carnage and chaos of the men under attack.

Baldwin grasped for the sword on his hip and tried to stand, but Ralf kept a grip firmly on him, holding him tight to the rocky earth that began to soften with the fluids of men.

Let me stand, Ralf, Baldwin said, trying to suppress any emotion he felt, trying to sound braver than he knew himself to be. Let me go fight these cowards who have slain our brothers!

Do you see these cowards? Look about you, boy: Where are the legions who fire upon us? Where are the echoes of their battle cry? They cannot be found! Not here! They wait for us to let down our guard once more, and then they shall attack again. To rise now is folly. Do not do their work for them. If you are to die today, on this god-forsaken ground, do not give them aid – make them earn your life; make them pay tenfold what it is worth to you!

There was a fire in Ralf's eyes as he spoke these words. A fire that burned over the grave of sadness that Baldwin had seen being dug there for several seasons. In the heat of battle, this was the Ralf that Baldwin had seen years before, the Ralf who knew war as a priest knew the word of God.

Baldwin pulled himself from the steel gaze of the man he knew again and surveyed the ridges with his own eyes. True enough, no enemy stood above them. There were no men giving charge, calling to whatever gods they knew to protect them and give will to slaughter their enemies. Apart from the moans of those who had fallen to the initial assault, all may well have been as it was before the first arrow had found its mark.

So what do we do? Wait here for them to come and kill us as we cower?

Ralf looked at Baldwin the way a one would look at an unwell child who could barely grasp the color of cloth, let alone the world at large. Aye, we wait, he said, but we don't cower, and we don't wait to die. We wait for time and death to be on our side. We wait for them.

The thought of waiting for attack and death did not sit well with the impetuous young man. Looking about him, though, he saw no others attempting to do anything more. He knew his place; he knew to do as was told.

Together, the men waited.

Baldwin could see that the knight riding down the ranks was Elias, the King's most trusted. He rode down to them from the end of the place of death where the army had been waiting, hunkered low. From the distance, he could hear the knight shouting words to the men as he made his way about them, but he could not hear responses being offered.

The boy closed his eyes. Struggled to shut out the sounds of his breath and his heart. What words was Elias giving to the men who cowered on the rocks like crabs hiding from gulls? Surely, he was telling them that this was not the behavior of men, let alone soldiers who served the King. He must be reminding them of their place, their duty, their allegiance. He would muster within them the courage that had escaped them all. The courage that had escaped even the steadfast Ralf. Elias would call them to their feet and call them to battle, and in battle they could hope to regain the glory that they had lost while shrinking as men within the spilled blood of their comrades. Perhaps the great knight would lead them up the slopes to meet their enemy, face to face. He would show them valor and nobility.

Elias's words were still too far for Baldwin to hear. He opened his eyes and looked for the knight. He looked for the hope that the great man would bring the quivering ranks that surrounded him.

The fool, Ralf said.

What fool can he be? He is a great and noble knight, and he calls these men to their feet to fight with him, for the King!

Baldwin felt a steady rage build within him as he stayed with Ralf. Ralf, the man he had held in such high regard, now cowering next to corpses and rocks, too afraid to fight further. This was no man, Baldwin thought. This was simply a child who had gone off to play war and no longer wished to get dirty.

He can be a fool, the calm voice asserted, if he can only attain his nobility through what he deems to be a noble death.

Ralf pointed towards the knight, sitting high on his horse, shouting as he marched down the line. Baldwin followed the gaze, and watched as the first arrow hit Elias in the shoulder, causing him to stop. The second caught him just under the chin but a moment later.

From the distance, Baldwin thought he could see bewilderment in the eyes of the knight as his hands clasped round his throat, releasing the reins of the horse the carried him. The blood trickled between his fingers as he began to slump. When the third arrow struck his back, the knight responding by sitting higher than before, chest thrust before him, body tensing to the newfound pain near his spine.

His horse, sensing the need of its rider, jerked forward in an effort to escape, only forcing the knight from it, before it too felt the sting of the enemy's arrows.

Baldwin watched both rider and horse succumb to a barrage.

Hitting the knight with such ease, why have they not fired upon us? Baldwin asked, breaking his gaze from the killing.

Perhaps you should ask the enemy what it is to be noble, was the only reply that Ralf would offer.

The true attack finally came, behind a last wave of arrows that fell like rain, so blindly fired that the desire seemed only to be awe and terror rather than true effectiveness. Still, terror was as an effective a weapon as any carried by an army.

The first of the enemy appeared on the ridge where the sun had risen. The second appeared on the ridge where it would soon set. Baldwin felt his heart quicken and his palms sweat as he realized what the enemy wanted them to know: They were surrounded on both sides. This gorge would be a grave for the assembled mass.

It's time, Ralf said.

The old soldier stood, bringing out his sword. The weapon looked much like Ralf, though less rough on the edges where he had sharpened it. This edge caught the light of the sun, and for a moment Baldwin found himself blinded. As his sight returned, the other soldiers, cowards in the eyes of the boy only minutes before, stood and joined the old war-dog. Baldwin found himself to be the last to rise.

The battle call travelled down the line, and when the men near him began their scream, Baldwin released all of the air within his lungs, adding his own voice to the single voice of the army. With them, he raised his sword; the normal, cumbersome weight of the blade seemingly absent as the strength for war found its way into him.

As the call died, it was returned from both sides as the enemy swarmed the ridges like ants leaving their hill. The number of enemy was easily two-to-one greater than the army of the King. Still, there was no panic amongst the men trapped within the gorge. Even the fear that had momentarily gripped every fifth man, Baldwin included, seemed evaporated in the hot sun. There was only rage for the murder of their brothers, whose bodies remained in repose on the ground that would soon see more blood than it could have ever been meant to, and excitement for the coming victory.

Keep your back to mine, Ralf said, and do not forget who is yours and who is theirs. Fight strong, fight with honor, and fight for your brothers; never for yourself. Fight so we all see tomorrow and you will find your way to our fire tonight. If you do not journey there, then we shall see you on the boat, or in the green fields beyond the river.

Baldwin felt the old soldier's elbow hit his, and he returned the motion.

For valor, for king, for brothers, for honor, Baldwin heard himself saying. For tomorrow, if not for me, for the next man.

The enemy came down upon them in one fell swoop.

The camp was solemn that night. The King and his knights, save the one who had been buried, grave marked by shield and flame, remained in their tent, and there was little revelry to be found around the fires.

At Baldwin's circle, a man had produced a lute, but the scowls he received before he could pluck a single string caused him to hide it once more. Only grunts could be heard between the slurping of the night's stew, which was little more than muddy water.

This journey the army was on was seemingly endless, now. No longer did the men feel as though they were fighting a war. War had purpose and a desired outcome. There was no purpose here. The men were fighting battles with no cause or reason behind them. Surely, they had travelled through every country that posed any threat or value, and now found themselves in lands that none had even known to exist.

For what did they ride?

For what did they fight?

The King kept only quarters with his knights these nights, who, in turn, only pointed the men where they needed to go. No longer did they fight men who spoke in languages they understood, nor did they fight men whose tongues spoke languages they were familiar with, so they could not even ask their enemy what these battles were about; learn what was to be gained by one side and lost by another.

We are men of war, Geoffrey said, breaking the silence. Men of war, and nothing more.

Eyes fell upon him, and he kept his only eye on his stew, watching something black float about in it that did not seem as though it belonged.

Silence returned, and it passed amongst the men, who waited to see if Geoffrey would say more. It was considered that he was no longer the same man since he lost his eye, and that his thoughts seemed to lurk in the darker places that most men prefer to believe cannot exist within the caverns of their minds. It would seem, as his silence continued, that he had simply let loose with one of the thoughts that lurked in this recessed darkness. And the men would let it stay at that, until he spoke again; We march and we kill, without reason or cause. We burn villages and slaughter those who oppose us without care or concern. We fight because we are told to, not because there is a need to.

Would you rather they kill us, instead, Geoffrey? One man said, voice raised with either anger at the words being spoken, or fear that these words contained truth.

They fight us because we invade their homeland, Geoffrey said, keeping his voice flat. Would you not fight a man – an army – that invaded yours? Would you not try to defend what is yours by rights from those who would take it from you by force?

He looked up from his stew, face somber, but thoughtful, and continued, They know that we are here only to take from them, but do we know why we take from them? We ride only to conquer. We march only for war. It would seem, then, that we are only men of war, for that is now all that we seem to know.

More silence ensued before another man said, We are soldiers. Of course we are man of war!

Half-hearted grunts and nods of acknowledgment came from those gathered. Men looked to one another, murmuring their shared belief of that fact, even if the belief was wavering. Baldwin and Ralf, however, kept their eyes on Geoffrey, whose gaze had returned to his pottage.

Are we soldiers? Geoffrey asked. I do not recall having been born a soldier, with sword and shield in hand. Prior to this life, I remember that I was a farmer. I existed to sow and harvest to feed my family and my village. It was not my duty then to kill another soul. Can none of you say the same? Were you all spat from the gashes of your mothers carrying blades and crying for battle instead of her breast?

The murmurs ceased, and the men stopped looking at one another, and instead found themselves looking at the rock that existed at their feet.

I, said one, was a baker.

I a poet, said another.

Slowly, all of the men said what it was that had occupied them before they had come to this army, fighting for His Majesty. All, save Ralf, whose lack of voice in the matter was louder than all of the other men combined.

What did you do, Ralf, before all of this? Baldwin asked, unsure of whether or not speaking the words was worse than hearing the answer.

Ralf gazed at the young man through the flames, now weathered and torn by war from marching with him these years. He wondered about Baldwin, and if he would ever leave this army and go back to the life that he left behind, or if he would die here, or on some other distant field of battle with countless others, his name fading from history like sand pulled from the beach by a receding wave. Could he still believe those words he had once said to the King, or did he now understand the words the King had given him in return?

What would keep someone such as that here?

Ralf sighed, and broke his gaze. War, he said, is all I know.

And with that, Ralf left the fire, heading off to find his own peace in the throes of the night, not that he could ever hope find it there. Solemnly, as though watching a funeral procession, the other men watched him walk away. Even Geoffrey felt compelled to observe as the shadow crept from the fire, disappearing into the darkness.

Not one among them spoke again before light.

The wolf had been howling from the top of the ridge without pause for several minutes. The sound had pulled the man from his sleep, and he set out to see what Tristan was alerting him to. Before leaving, he gave a look to his meager camp, deciding it best tear it down before heading after the animal.

He made sure the fire was out, and gathered his weapons and utensils. Each time he went through this act, he realized, if not fully, how little he truly had in this world. Were he to die in this moment, on this ground, as the grey of the predawn washed over him, his breath hanging, all he would leave behind would be but these meager samplings of what one would dare call a life. In time, the remnants would fade, as would his body, having been left to the elements, unburied and unmourned.

The air was cold on his face. As the wolf continued to howl, the man thought of his life. The things he had seen. The people he now missed. He looked to the sound of Tristan, knowing the animal was not too far off, letting this clear his head of the burdens of regret. He could not see the creature through the morning fog, but knew he was at the top of the ridge, above the trees, by how the sound carried.

Surveying the camp before taking down the last of it and going after the howls of the wolf, he saw her standing at the edge of the trees. Her soft, blue dress clung to her body in the moisture. Her hair was slack, as was her spirit. She did not take her eyes off of him, and neither he her. Badly, the man wanted to go to her, and to walk with her amongst the trees; to leave this tattered life behind.

He could see them together, so easily. The cottage would be warm. From the window, she would watch him venture to the woods to hunt, or chop wood for the fire. Occasionally, they would go to town to trade for goods. Their life together would be long and simple. They would grow old and die in the comfort of home. Side-by-side, they would be buried. Then, they would be eternal.

Tristan's call brought him from this waking dream. Looking back to the trees, the man saw that she was gone. He was still alone.

No longer could he care about this place; this land he found himself wandering. There was no home here, just as there had been no home out in war. The world continued to change, but he could change with it no more than he could change the past he so desperately clung to while trying to escape it in the same breath.

He finished breaking down his camp, and set off after the infernal black beast.

By the time he reached the ridge, the wolf had run off. The man had heard the animal offer a single bark, and then silence. Just as well, he thought, he was feeling frustrated and may take it out on the burdensome creature.

He stood there, above the trees, looking out into the mist. There was little to discern, just a clearing that, through gaps in the fog, seemed to stretch on. His feet felt cold as he sunk slightly into the moist earth, and his breath came with a little pain from the hike. The world was taking a toll on him. So be it, he thought. Let it have him.

What did you see, you ill begotten dog?

Eyes unflinching, he peered further into the grey world that rolled out before and beneath him. He knew that there must be something out there to have caught Tristan's attention in such a way. Soon, the sun would rise and burn through this mist, and he would then know what lurked deep in the mystery; or perhaps it would find him first.

The man closed his eyes and inhaled deeply. The air was thick and pungent with wet. He could smell the moss and leaf of the wood. Gas from the bog he had meandered through two days ago reached him as well, the stench rising from that which he wore, locked into each fiber and hair. Beyond that, though, there was something else. He inhaled once more, sorting through the scents.

Smoke. Smoke carrying through thick, wet air, and finding its way to him.

So, Tristan, you found fire, he thought, but in this damp, what, I wonder, could be the cause?

He crouched lower on the ridge, and waited for the fog to burn away so that he would have his answer.

The sun came. The fog left. The man had been dreaming on the ridge. As the warmth struck him, he opened his eyes. The world was a blur as it slowly came back to him. He blinked away the dream, and soon saw the green pasture before him, brighter now than it had been before. Though some was natural in form, most had been taken from the forest. Stumps had clearly been pulled from the earth after trees had been felled to make room for more field space. This was farmland.

Looking further across the pasture, he could see the remnants of the small village. The buildings were nothing more than piles of blackened wood and stone, occasional tufts of virgin thatch somehow still appearing; but the flames of the fire that had decimated the place having since been extinguished by the damp embrace of Time and Earth. Tendrils of smoke still rose in spots, but no orange flame remained; nor, that he could make out from his vantage point, did any signs of the life that once must have thrived in this place. Whatever had happened here was now over.

Across the way, on the other side of the smoldering huts and homes, at the tree line, the wolf stared at him. Barely a black speck, Tristan's eyes still shone across the distance.

The man stood slowly, body groaning and creaking. Ensuring all about him was secure, he set off, down into field.

Walking through the burned out shells that were all that remained of the lives the villagers once had, he kept his hand firm on the grip of his blade. He was certain no soul remained in this place, but he could not be too sure of that fact. He thought of a gorge in some foreign landscape, where an army thought they marched alone, and had sorrowfully been proven wrong. Better to stay alert to all possibilities, the man had learned, than it was to simply hope for the best.

Each blackened window he passed, he stuck in his head. The air in all of the places was still thick with wet smoke, but that was all. No flame, no man, no woman, no child. No life. The place was dead and empty, all having fled in the night, if not before. Still, unease lingered within him. Something about the place seemed unnatural at best; unholy at worst.

Each step the man took was measured. Though there could be no more than seven buildings, all relatively near to each other, he took his time. Though stones could go unturned, his curiosity about this place needed to be quelled.

Stepping around an empty cart, he found the first sign that there had once been life in this place. A dog lay dead near the wheel, eyes open, tongue lolled, chest collapsed. Perhaps, the man thought, in a panic someone had crushed the poor animal. How long ago had it been?

He could see no swelling or decay about the carcass of the wretched beast, and in the cold the flies had yet to find it. Stooping, he pressed his hand into the matted, brown fur. Sure enough, the animal was dead. Dead, and cold. Whatever had happened to it had not occurred too recently, but easily since the sun had set the previous night. Maybe only five or six hours.

The man stroked the fur with care, a sense of sorrow for the poor animal filling him.

He resumed his search.

It came to be that the last building gave him the answer he was looking for. Through the window, he could see the corpses. There were seven of them, charred and placed in line on the floor. The flesh on each was cracked and black, and they were no longer whole. Parts of the bodies had crumbled into ask, lost amongst the dust of the burnt thatch that was once the roof.

The man pulled himself from the window and walked to the door, burned away, only bits of blackened wood remaining, where he found the eighth corpse. The poor soul, it seemed, had tried to claw its way from the fire. A single arm, from hand to just beyond torso, unburned, reached beyond the threshold and into the world outside. Seeing the arm, the man recoiled in horror.

A soldier, he had witnessed much that man could to do each other, including immolation of another person. A burned arm by itself is not what frightened him, for much worse had been witnessed in his life. What caused him to slowly back away, then quickly move from the burned buildings and towards the wood where the wolf awaited, was the sight of the lesion in the pit of the arm that leaked the pus.

Plague had found the village. Plague, and he had found himself walking amongst a place it had decimated.

In the woods, he vomited all that was in his stomach. A panic filled him that he had never known in battle, only before. Only once in his life.

How could he not know the signs? How could he allow the wolf to lead him into such darkness? The Devil himself could not be so cruel!

He thought about what had just happened. Did he touch anything but his sword and the crushed dog? Might he have had contact with something that could still be cursed with the death? He closed his eyes, reviewed his steps, and was sure he had not touched a building with his hand. Certainly, he had not touched the arm that was still riddled with the curse.

Behind those closed eyes, he could see it so clearly, the limb. Fingertips black, half-buried in the earth. Skin pale and soft, the arm of a woman. The arm still attached to a burned torso. The fire had not reached this upper-quarter of the body. Head and all else blackened and crisp. Just the arm, the pit, and only a little more.

These remnants should be burned. He knew this. He knew that he should go back and give a final flame to that which remained in that building. He could not bring himself to do this, though. He could not guarantee his own safety were he to venture back to a place of such death. It did not matter, anyway. So remote was the place, the road only travelled by those who lived here, that no risk or worry existed that those unfamiliar with the death that had blanketed the village would stumble across it.

Once more he vomited. Through the trees, he could see the black fur waiting for him ahead. Steading his hands, he went towards it, simply because he had no other option.

That night, sleep refused to find him easily. He stared into the fire he had built, allowing his stew to grow cold within its bowl as he did so. His stomach anguished for nourishment, but he ignored the cries. The brush with his mortality had hit him hard. Through the battles, he had seen death. He had come to know that which came for all men. But to him, this was different. In battle, he could accept that he would fall to the blade or point of the enemy. He would fight, and perhaps his life would end in glory or in unimportance. Still, it would end, and likely quickly and with little pain.

This plague was not the same as death on the field of battle. Plague would cause time to stop for him. If he was lucky, death would take him within two days. He had heard people surviving as long as a week, though. How could he ever endure that? When would he even know it had ended? Such pain and misery before succumbing to something not an enemy, just purely unknown? A living death.

This is the thought that kept him from sleeping. Not a thought of death, but a thought of life, if it could be called that, ending in absolute misery.

He found that night to be among the longest he had ever known.

VI

The wolf watched the man as he finally slept, the first rays of dawn having just begun to creep into the sky. It kept its distance from the sleeping figure. The stench of death lingered on the man more than it ever had before, and the wolf knew that all men were most dangerous near the end. In such moments, man could lash out without cause or reason. Though the wolf felt no real sense of loyalty to this man it had found and followed for weeks, there was a slight sense of companionship that had grown from its initial curiosity. Here was a man, alone and in the wood. He hunted like other men, walked as they did, and made fire to cook food the same; yet, there had seemed to be something more to him.

The wolf knew what that different thing was. The man had spent a great deal of time in the presence of death. He had likely caused the specter to visit itself upon others earlier than had been planned by the universe. He was no stranger to the fear that was the next life, for he very nearly walked with one leg within that realm; and though death had not ridden on the man's back when the wolf first found him, it certainly sat beside him now as he slept beneath his furs, next to dying embers.

The glow of life that had been about the man was fading, and that light would be snuffed within the week; of this the wolf was sure. The animal felt neither pity nor sorrow at the impending demise of this creature it had observed; instead, the flame of its curiosity was rekindled. As it had watched the man live these past weeks, so to would it watch the man die.

The wolf walked through the wood, padded feet barely touching the moss as it stalked the rabbit. The animal stayed close to the man's camp these times, but it still had its own needs. Hunger had found it, and it sought to end those pangs before they drove it to feast upon the dying man, who already seemed too weak to put up much defense against an attack. Still, whatever it was that was claiming the man could surely claim the wolf, as well. The animal knew that only in the madness of starvation would it risk bringing such a fate upon itself. Better to crush the feeling now before it grew to that point of desperation.

As it moved among the wet leaves, allowing the moisture to slick its matted fur, the wolf kept its nose above the moss, nostrils flared. Each breath was analyzed for the scent of the grey rabbit that had made the mistake of being seen. Had the wolf not watched it bound through a shrub, the rabbit could have had a greater head start before the predator caught the scent. So often, though, the fates were cruel to the careless, and so the wolf had given calculating chase.

Inhaling here, the wolf knew to turn round the next tree. Inhaling there, it knew not to go under the log where the tracks seemed to lead, but instead go the opposite direction.

Once there, another breath gave news that the hunt was nearing an end. The rabbit was close. The wolf paused, pawing at the moss to release the scent of the frightened animal it was stalking, whose day had begun with the promise of life renewed, but would now end in the promise of life for another. Predator and prey; a dance eternal.

The moss told the wolf the animal was there. The scent was fresh. So fresh, the wolf began to salivate. It could already taste the game it hunted.

Turning in circles, nose so near the ground that the wolf would suffocate were he to push down further, the animal sniffed every area of the small clearing. Perking its ears, it could hear the thunder of the rabbit's heartbeat. The small animal was, without doubt, frightened, but the wolf did not have the time nor want to care about such things. All it cared about was catching its prey and savoring the coming meal that would follow the close of the hunt.

A final inhalation and the wolf stopped turning. It pulled back its ears and peered into the darkness of the hole the rabbit had sought shelter in, bearing its teeth with a growl. The rabbit's heart quickened more so, to the point that the wolf, if not for experience in these matters, would have thought it to the point of giving out. Deliberately, the wolf moved forward, eyes not leaving the black void where the rabbit waited for its demise. The predator knew better than to even blink, lest the prey seize the opportunity to run from its shelter and back into the wood, where the wolf may hold no hope of catching it.

Each of the wolf's breaths came with a heavy, menacing growl, designed to keep the rabbit in its place. By sound and scent, the wolf knew that it would be able to thrust its head into the hole and grab the rabbit with relative ease. Each step forward, the wolf examined the coming kill within its head, all thought of the dying man pushed aside in this primordial moment. It would grab the rabbit by whatever fur and flesh it could easily reach, and the small creature would squeal in a final attempt to ward off the attack. Too late to escape, the wolf would snap the rabbit's neck with shakes, and then the meal would commence. The rabbit would be dead, the wolf's stomach would be full. Such was nature; the nature of the hunter, the nature of the hunted, the nature of the world.

When the wolf's head finally entered the rabbit's futile hiding place, its prey knew that there was no chance to be had.

It was all over quickly.

A cry from the man in the night pulled the wolf from its sleep, and it dared to venture closer to the huddled mass that puffed shuddered breaths into the darkness.

Don't leave me! The man screamed into the night.

The wolf stayed behind the man, not wanting to frighten him. What was this man screaming about? To whom was he speaking? Though the wolf was used to the man speaking to it as though it were another human, even taking to calling it Tristan, these cries were directed at no one that seemed to be present. To be sure, the wolf looked around itself, but there was nothing else there. Even the few insects that could survive the wet and the cold of the winter months were gone from this place. The man had forsaken this part of the wood with his death. The two beings were surely alone.

Please, don't leave me... the man sobbed into the night, causing the wolf to perk its ears once more.

What noises were these? The wolf wondered as the man gasped and shuddered. It had yet to hear the man cry, and so was worried that this was something new; either with the death, or with the man. Though curious still about what was occurring, trepidation still lingered within the animal.

Death was heavy in the air the man breathed, but that made him no less dangerous than he was previously.

The man fell silent, though his body continued to heave. Such strength showing through such weakness, the wolf thought of the man. In these three days, the man had barely been able to move. His fingers had turned black, and he neither ate nor drank. He had even gone without the warmth of a fire at night. The wolf knew that man could not endure like this, so weak the species was; and yet this one refused to give in to the embrace of a death that rescued all who suffered in the clutches of life. The strength was seemingly unnatural. At times, when the man would sit upright as if poked with a sharp object, the wolf would worry that it had been wrong, and that the man had only given a ruse to try and catch the animal. But as soon as the man would rise, he would fall back down, and go for hours without movement, the only indication of life being the raspy sound of his breathing. Labored and wet, the wolf knew that whatever sickness adorned the man in this cold wood had spread into his lungs.

Death, the animal was certain, would come for the man before the sun set on the next day. The wolf could wait that long before leaving the edge of the clearing to hunt and drink.

Dawn came, and the man still lingered in this life. The wolf had not slept after being awoken in the night. Time was short for the man, and it was no harm to the wolf to sacrifice some of its own to time to be with him in the end.

It had circled the clearing and sat near the man's sightlines, though the animal had been wise enough to keep just beyond them, lest the man become frightened or angry. It had seen strength return to the man, if only for moments, throughout the course of this death, and it remembered the rage the man had directed towards it when he finalized realized a sickness had found him. The rocks and sticks the man had hurled at the wolf. The arrows that had landed not far from where it had huddled, frightened but unwavering in its interest. There was no need to suffer through any of that, again, the wolf thought.

The wolf tracked the man's gaze to a point just beyond the trees. Though the wolf could not see what the man was staring at, he could see the gaze was not lost and bumbling. The man was focused on something and refused to break his stare. Slowly, as if pulled upon by an outside force, the man rose to a near seated position, arms reaching out to whatever it was he saw.

Worried for its own safety, the wolf slowly backed away on its haunches, further from the man's line of sight. It kept its ears up for any alerting noises, and tail low, between its legs. The animal made ready to run deep into the woods if the need presented itself; but after a few heartbeats, it saw there would be no need.

The man did not see him. Even if he could, the strength to do much more than stare at the animal who kept him company had long ago abandoned him.

The man's arm trembled as he grasped at the air, beckoning what he saw to come to him. His mouth moved slowly, looking as though he was chewing on sand. The wolf listened, but no sounds came forth. The man, it seemed, could no longer speak. All that reached the wolf was the smell of excrement and death, defeat and sorrow.

After a time, the man lay back down, huddling for warmth, the gleam of sweat that coated his flesh more noticeable in the light. The fever had fully set in, burning away the life. Surely, the wolf thought, this man knew that his time had come. Why did he bother to fight? No creature could forever outrun the infinite reach of death. What would cause this man to think he was any different?

The wolf lay on the ground, resting its chin upon its outstretched paws, contemplating this man that was before it, ever curious as to his nature. It had seen many men, prior to its encounter with this one, and believed it would see many more in the seasons to come. Yet, this one, this solitary man who walked with head low, who moved without any sense of true purpose, seemed to be so different from those who had come before, and surely those who would come next. Though upright and clothed in the fur of other animals, the man seemed to the wolf to be so much like itself.

So odd was the notion that the wolf soon forgot it, and went back to just observing.

The man succumbed as the fog rolled back in. Midway through the day, he had begun to vomit blood that was as black as a river on a moonless night. These purging acts had taken a crippling toll on the man, and soon he was sapped of whatever strength that had managed to remain within him. No longer did he sit up, or even move. He just lay there, beneath the sun, wet breath slowly escaping him.

The wolf watched the hour of death come to a close as the man, with final effort, wiping blood and bile from his beard with the back of his hand, rose slowly to his feet. The wolf was no longer concerned, as the shadow that fell over the man was dark. This was the time of his end. There was no need to fear whatever may come.

The man stood shaky, unsure of the world around him. He pulled the sword that had been lying next to him up, and for a moment used it as a cane to steady himself further. His fingertips were black with what it was that infected him, his skin was drawn tight, and yellow pus ran from somewhere under his clothing, down his arm, and dripped from hand and finger to earth below. Though standing, swollen lungs struggling for air, each breath a raspy, raggedy mess, the man looked no more alive than corpses – man or animal – the wolf had set sight on before.

By sheer will, the man raised the sword, pointing the tip towards the woods, and let out a guttural cry that was all but pathetic, so heavy with the phlegm it had to cut through to exist. Still, the feeling was there, behind the sound. The power that had once run through the man went forth into the world in that final howl. The wolf felt as though the man may very well be trying to crack the world with his noise, and felt frightened and excited in the same instance. Such defiance in the face of death. Only man would act in a manner so futile. Only man would believe himself to be so worthy of an act.

The wood fell silent as the howl ceased.

The last of the man's strength was gone, carried in the currents over the trees and down the road. His grip on the sword failed, and the blade that had protected him through many a year and through countless battles fell to the soft ground, where it would remain for an age, overgrown and forgotten, steel becoming one with nature.

His arm falling to his side, the man gave a last look to the sky, eyes unable to see through the clouds that now covered them, before collapsing to his knees. No longer a man, the husk sat that way for a moment, before chin came to rest on chest, and arms, with fingers forever black and clutching, at side.

The man was no more.

Through the window of time, the wolf watched as the fragment that was once the man was reclaimed by the forest. Through seasons of winter and summer, fall and spring, the clothing and flesh slowly flaked away, and the bones collapsed. As the world moved on, new life growing from the forest floor as the old life died and gave nourishment back to the wood, even bone would turn to dust, and in the end, there would nothing left on the earth to mark the passing of the man who had wandered the world both solitary and with countless brothers. No kin remained to carry on his name into the great future. He would become lost to the ages, story untold, tales of his bravery and valor falling like the sand in the hourglass.

The wolf walked closer to the body, scent of death removed, smell of decay holding the air. It kept a distance; still, for whatever it was that had claimed the man may as well claim the beast. For a final time, the wolf lowered his head to the ground, smelling what remained of the presence of the man.

Turning away, without another glance, the animal returned to the wood, disappearing in the mist.

Afterword

Before anything else, I should first like to thank Nicole Nicolodemos for the invaluable service she provided in editing the story that you have just read. Often as I write, I find that I tend to skip words, sometimes entire sentences, in the frenzy at which I wish I advance the story (this in addition to any grammar, spelling, and punctuation errors that occur out of simple carelessness), and Nicole was kind enough, and patient enough, to review these words to ensure that as few errors as possible made it into the finished product that is *Man of War*. That which is done well is her; the rest is me.

Sincerely, Nicole, I thank you.

Also, I would like to give a few fond words of thanks to those who journeyed this far. Your devotion to this story means more than words can describe.

But what of *Man of War*... Where did it come from? How did it get here?

I wish I could answer these questions with concrete certainty, but I cannot. Like most things that I write, the basic idea for what you have read came to me out of the blue, but not in words. I found myself, as a night in October wore on, looking into my mind, and there I found the image of a grizzled, battle-weary soldier wrapped in firs staring out at a grey ocean with his cold eyes. Behind him, a wolf, forever wild, sat keeping a watchful eye of curiosity on the man who I would often refer to as The Soldier. This would serve to be genesis of the story, I suppose.

As I began to write a description of the image, the remainder of the soldier's journey began to flow forth, and within the week, I had completed the rough draft of his story. Several drafts later, the soldier's tale was final, and it is what you have just read.

Of course, there is more to this solitary figure than what you have just read, and I have thought long about what to include in his story; however, I decided that it bore little bearing to the tale told, and so it exists now solely within the halls and caverns of my mind. Will it ever be set free upon the world? I have my doubts, but the future forever remains unwritten.

Until then, as it were, a final thanks, and may you have your own journeys.

R.B.

Utah, December 2013

www.ingramcontent.com/pod-product-compliance
Lightning Source LLC
Chambersburg PA
CBHW072229190626
46809CB00017B/1540